AN ODD DOG CHRISTMAS

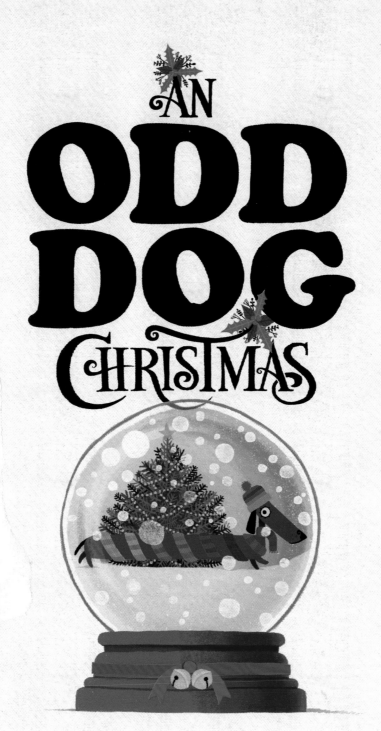

For Lynn and Adam

First published in hardback in the United Kingdom by HarperCollins *Children's Books* in 2021
This edition published in 2022

HarperCollins *Children's Books* is a division of HarperCollins*Publishers* Ltd
1 London Bridge Street, London SE1 9GF

www.harpercollins.co.uk

HarperCollins*Publishers*
1st Floor, Watermarque Building, Ringsend Road, Dublin 4, Ireland

978–0–00–841336–1

Text and illustrations copyright © Rob Biddulph 2021
Rob Biddulph asserts the moral right to be identified as the author/illustrator of the work.
A CIP catalogue record for this book is available from the British Library. All rights reserved.

Printed and bound in Italy

1 3 5 7 9 10 8 6 4 2

AN ODD DOG CHRISTMAS

Written and illustrated by

Rob Biddulph

HarperCollins *Children's Books*

For festive dogs
a festive day.

'Tis the
season
to spend
money

GET MORE
STUFF

It's Christmas Eve!
Hip hip hooray!

SNOW GLOBES

TREES

DECORATIONS

Singing!

Baking!

Wrapping!

Fun!

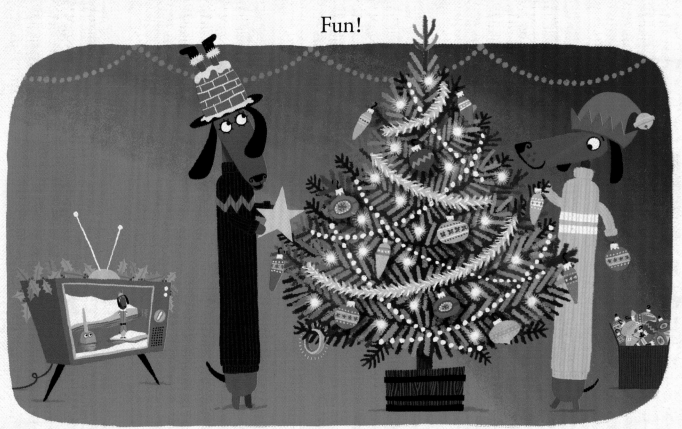

A merry time for everyone.

But wait. Look closer. Can you see
One dog behaving differently?

Someone on
this carousel

Is jingling a
different bell.

"I'm stumped," she sighs. "Confounded. Stuck.

I've shopped all day, but still no luck.

As Christmas Eve turns out its light,
She wanders through the silent night.

What's this?
A sign!
An arrow too!

STEP INTO
Christmas

She takes a breath...

...and walks straight through.

STEP INTO Christmas

STEP INTO
Christmas

"Well, bless my bones!
Is this a dream?

A winter wonderland
supreme!

With candy canes
and gingerbread...

And jolly elves
in green and red!"

But wait. Look closer. Can you see
Someone *not* feeling Christmassy?

A sniff. A cough. A loud "ATCHOO!".
This red-nosed reindeer's feeling... blue.

ATCHOO!

DASHER

"Poor thing," she says, "you don't look well.
You've got a sniffle – I can tell."

He blows his nose. He wipes his eyes.
"You're right," the poorly reindeer sighs.

"I hate to moan or cause a fuss
(Tonight's a special night for us)

But truth be told –" he turns away –
"I'm far too ill to pull the sleigh."

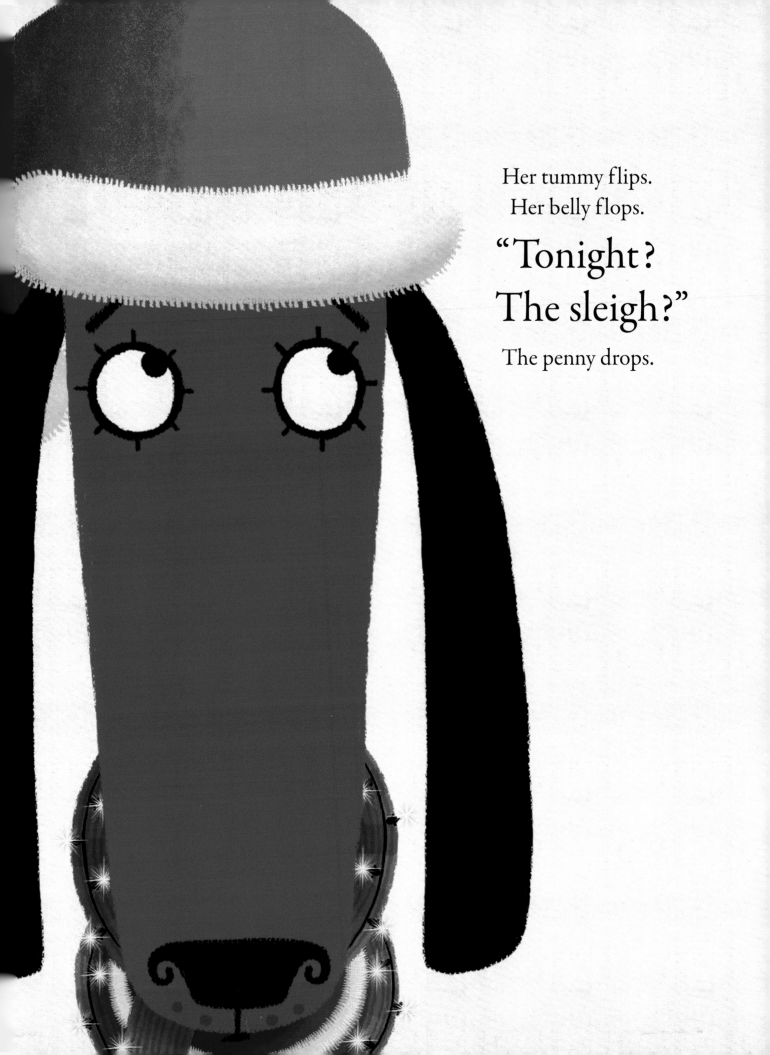

Her tummy flips.
Her belly flops.

"Tonight?
The sleigh?"

The penny drops.

They head back to the reindeer shed
And poor old Dasher goes to bed.

But then a warm voice, deep and clear,
Says...

"Welcome, friend.
I'm glad you're here."

"You see," declares the chap in red,
"We've got a busy night ahead.

And," says he, with worried frown,
"We are, it seems, a reindeer down..."

This dog, she does not hesitate.
She smiles a smile and stands up straight.

"I'm ready, Santa! What's the plan?
I'll help in any way I can."

And so, with Odd Dog flying high...

They blaze a trail across the sky.

Their busy night is at an end
And Odd Dog's thoughts
turn to her friend.

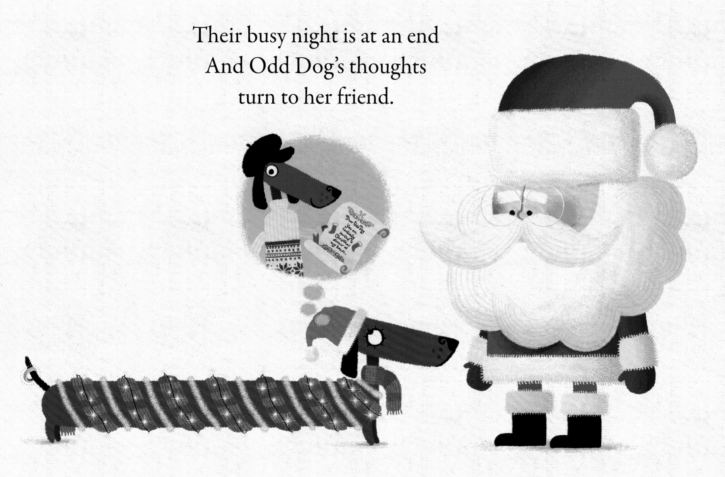

Santa smiles. "Here's my advice:
While toys and games are very nice,

A simple present from the heart
Is always the best place to start."

And just like that, it's crystal clear.

This dog has had a great idea.

For festive dogs a festive day
Of festive smiles and festive play.

Caring, sharing, friendship, fun.

Merry Christmas, everyone!

MAGIC
FLYING
DUST

Dear Dad Dog
thank you!
from Santa x